This activity book belongs to

____

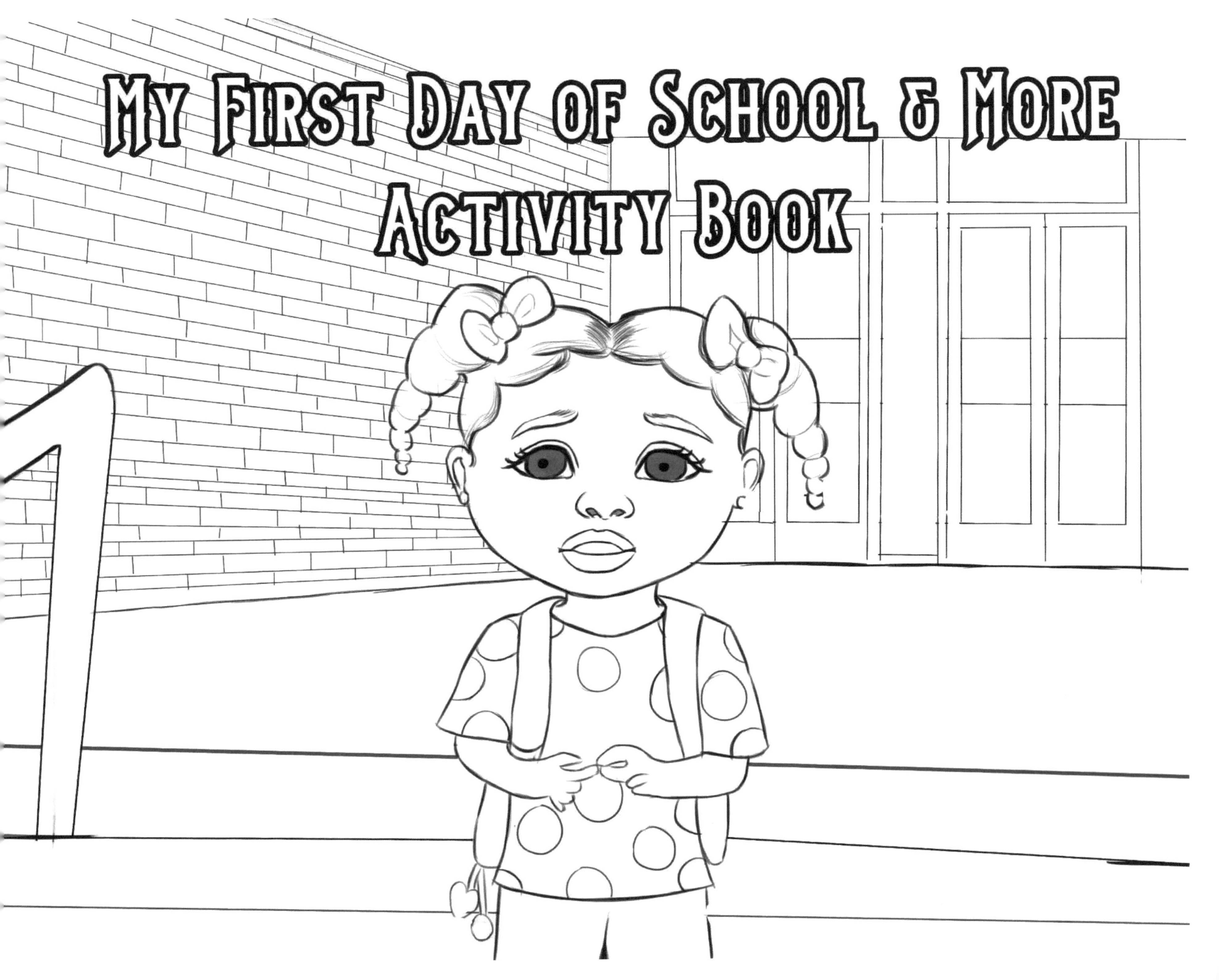
My First Day of School & More
Activity Book

Dr. Markethia Mull @ mmull@maminomull.com

My First Day of School & More Activity Book/Dr. Markethia Mull
Illustrations /Ochuko Eyaadah

Printed in the United States of America/Houston, TX

ISBN **979-8-9853160-5-6**

First Edition

Coloring Sheets

POPCORN
CHOCO CHIPS
Jellies
CUPCAKES
MOVIE STAR
HAPPY & ME

Ealia
Ealia
Ealia
Ealia

WELCOME TO KINDERGARTEN

Ms Young
August 22 2022
SHAPES
A
Apple
L
Lion
E
Hen
I
Pig
O
Box

FORREST HILLS ELEMENTARY SCHOOL

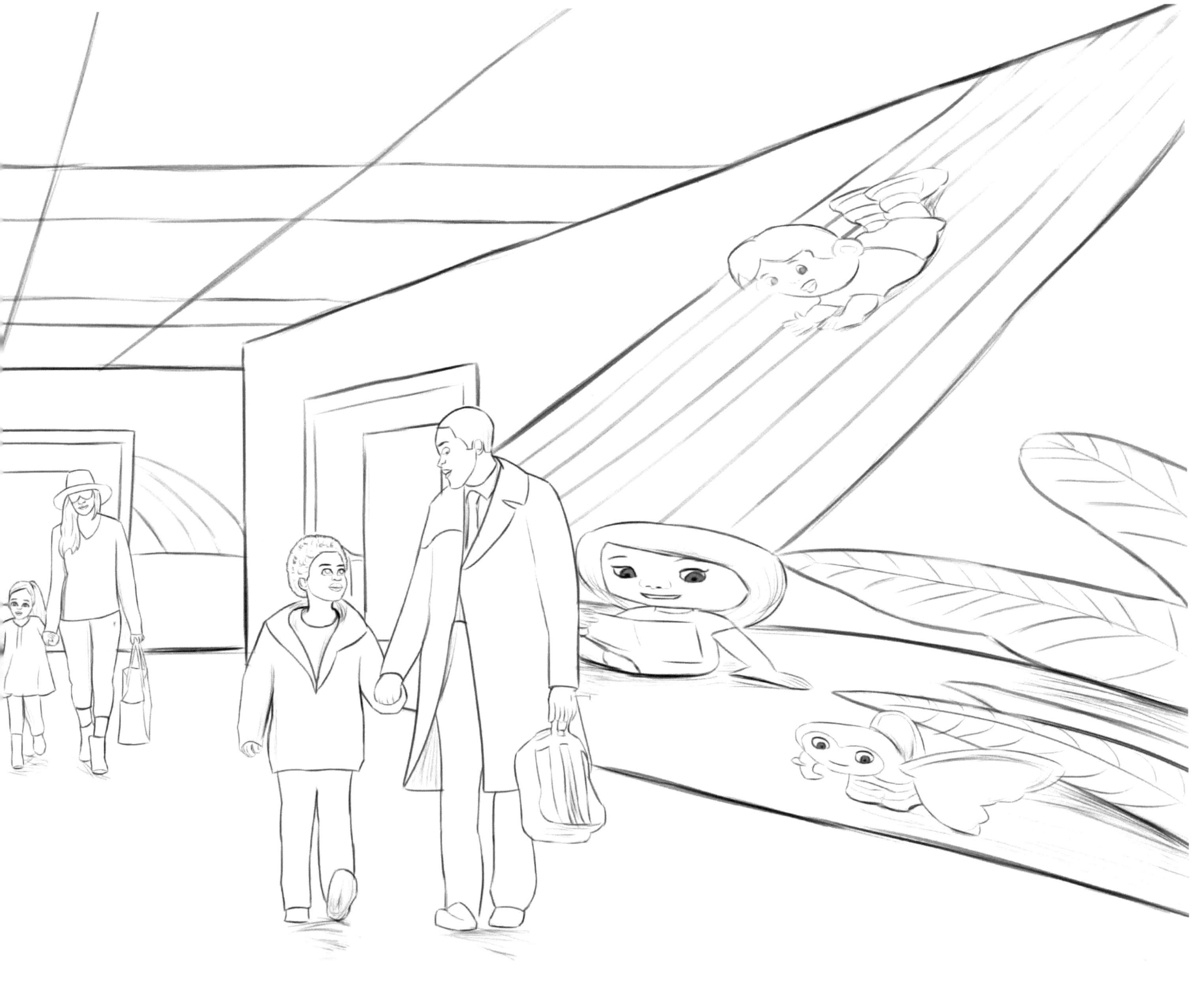

0 1
2 3
4 5
6 7

Let's Count!
1 2 3 4 5 6 7 8 9 10

A B C
a b c
NOW
AND L
1. ALL
2. THE ALF
3. READ ALO

WING
TOO!
T US
ET SONG
MY FIRST
FLUTTERS
POP CORN
POP CORN

Reading and Math Activities

Monday

Direction: Color each object that start with the letter Mm.

Mm

Trace the letters.

M

m

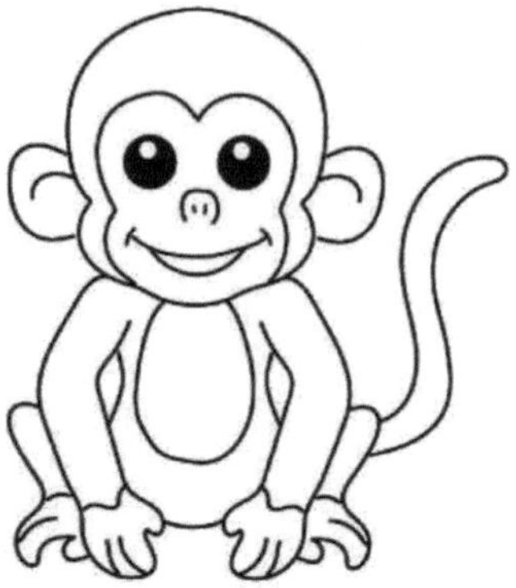

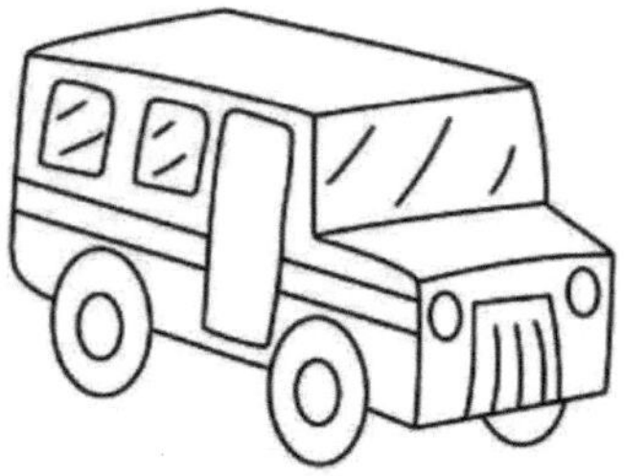

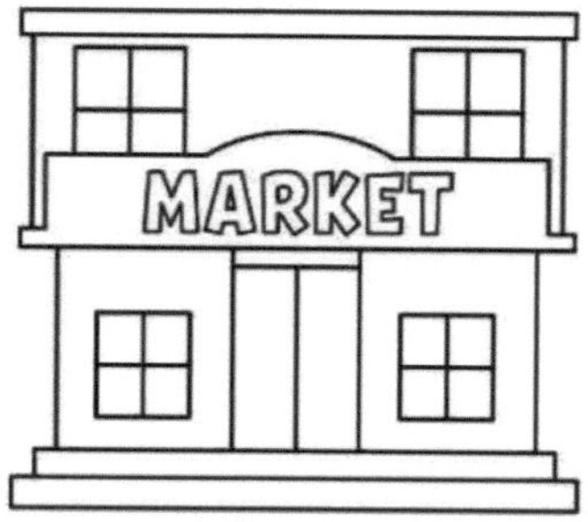

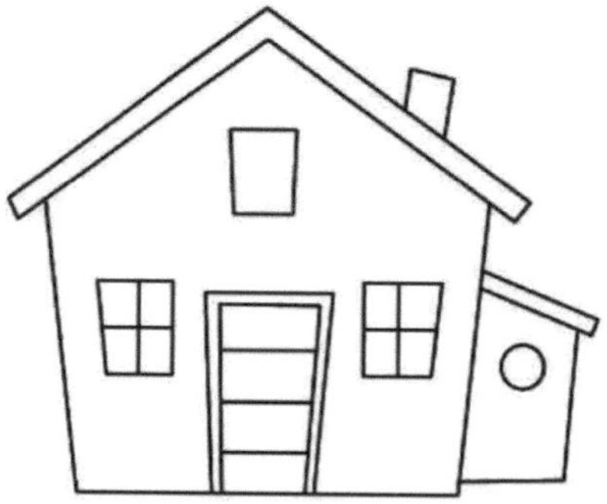

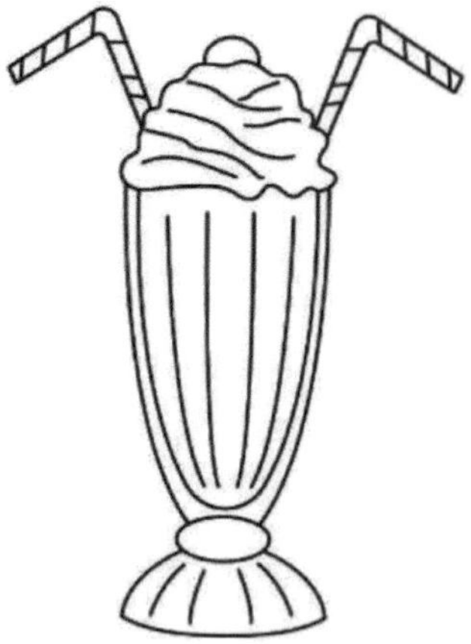

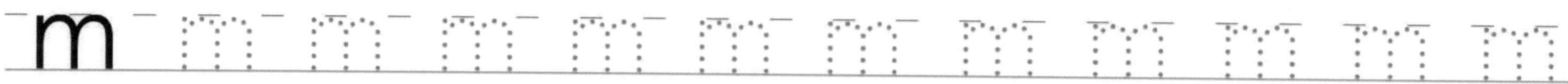

Monday

Direction: Color each object that start with the letter Aa.

Aa

Trace the letters.

A A A A A A A A A A A A

a a a a a a a a a a a a

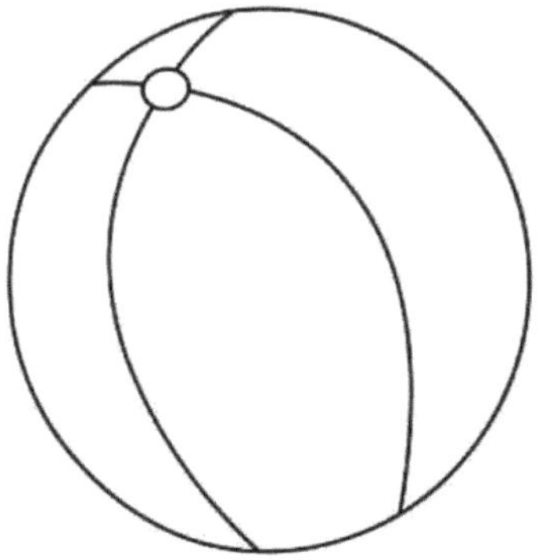

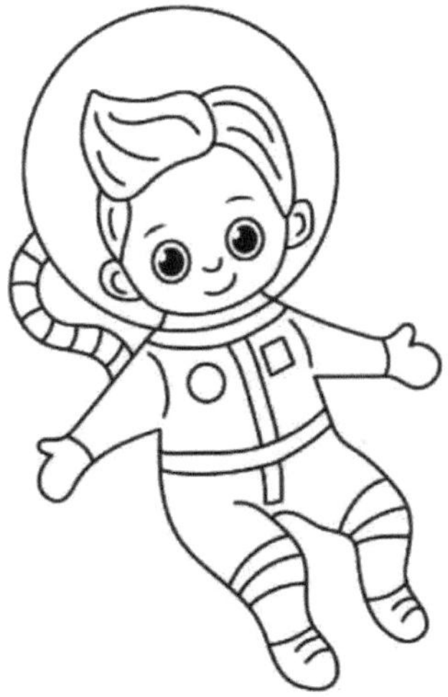

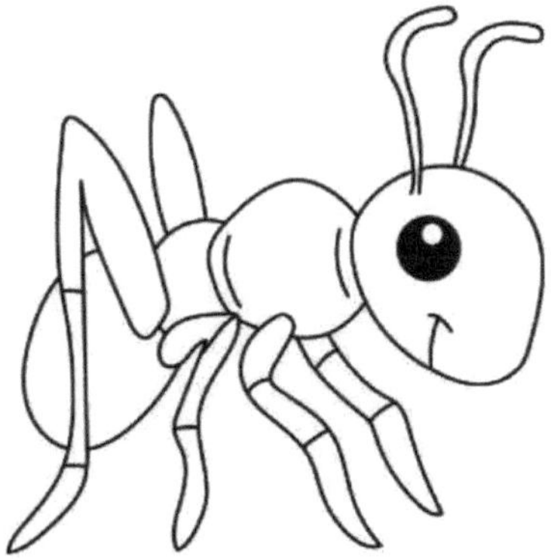

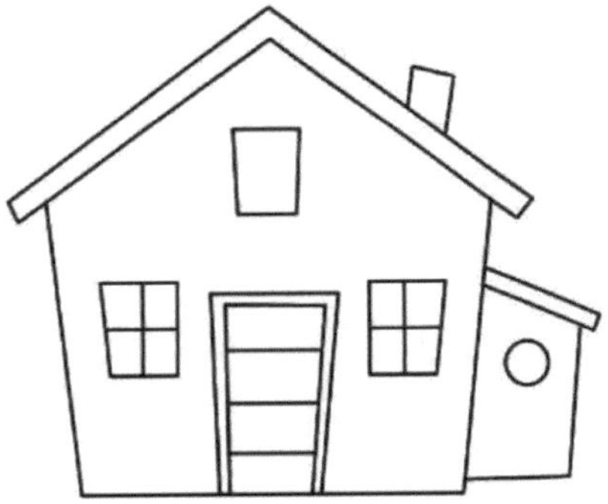

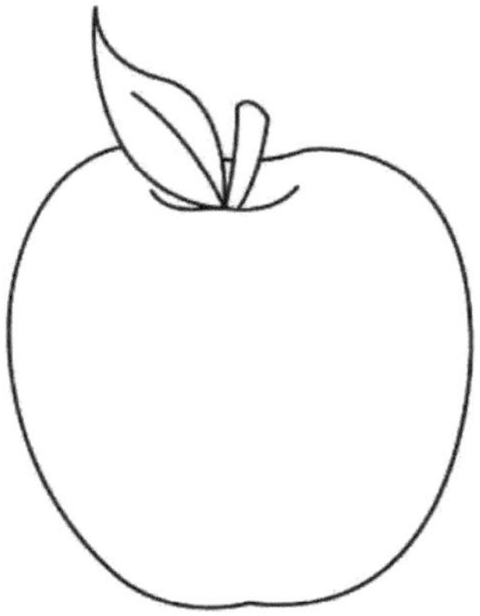

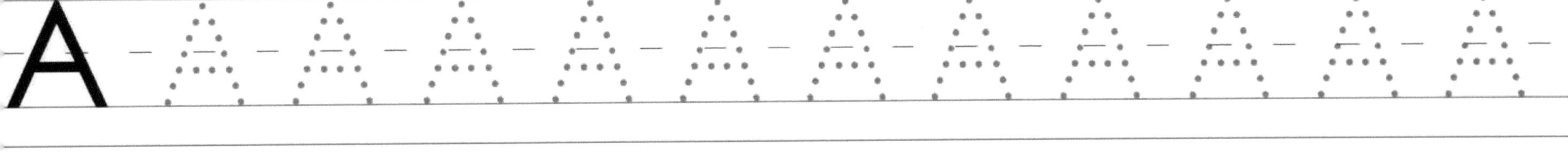

Tuesday

Direction: Color each object that start with the letter Ss.

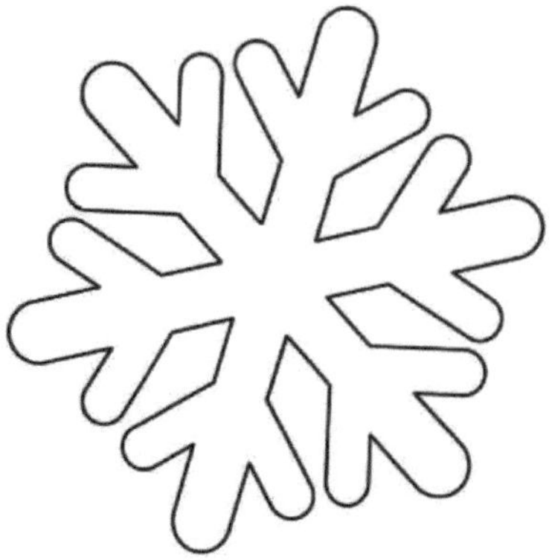

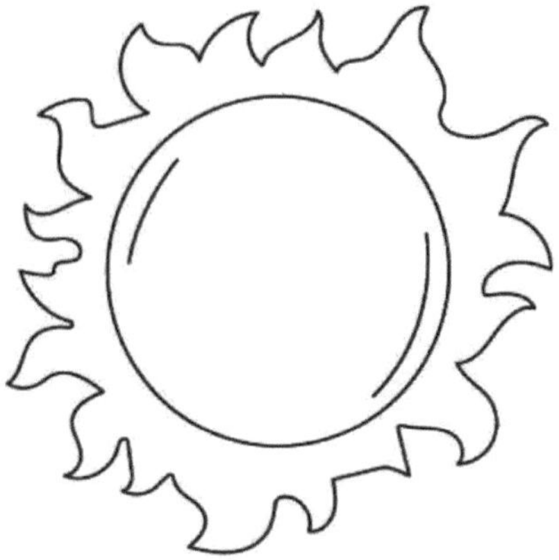

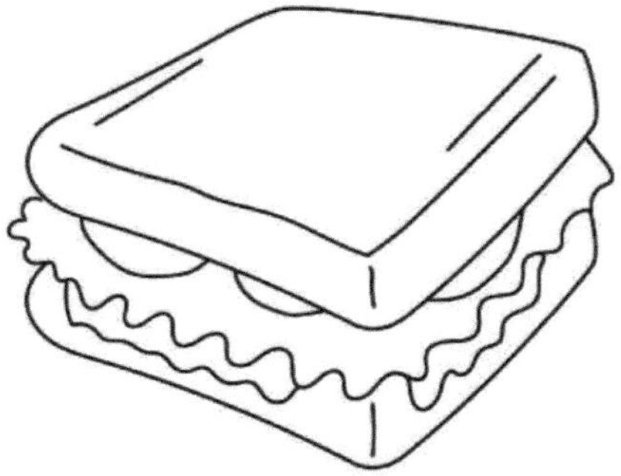

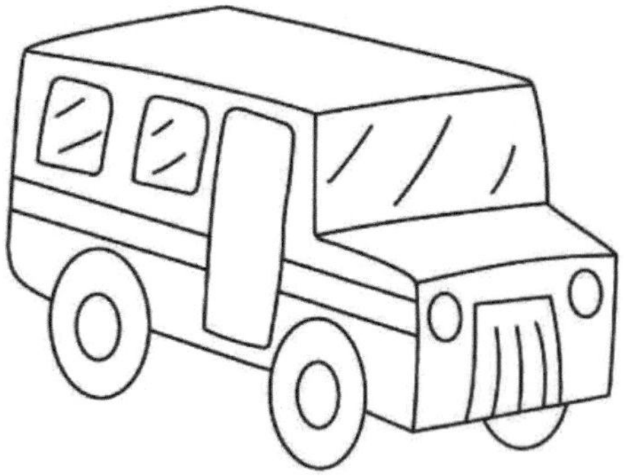

Trace the letters.

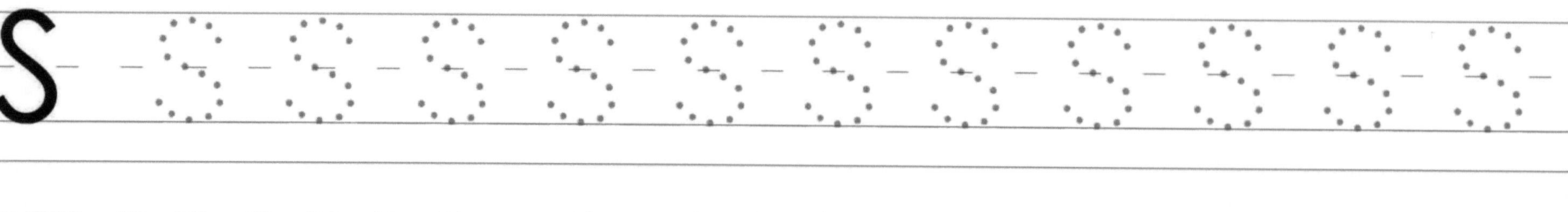

Tuesday

Direction: Color each object that start with the letter Ee.

Trace the letters.

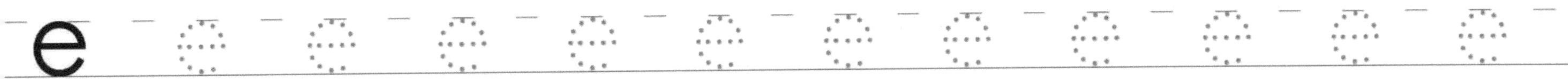

Wednesday

Direction: Color each object that start with the letter Rr.

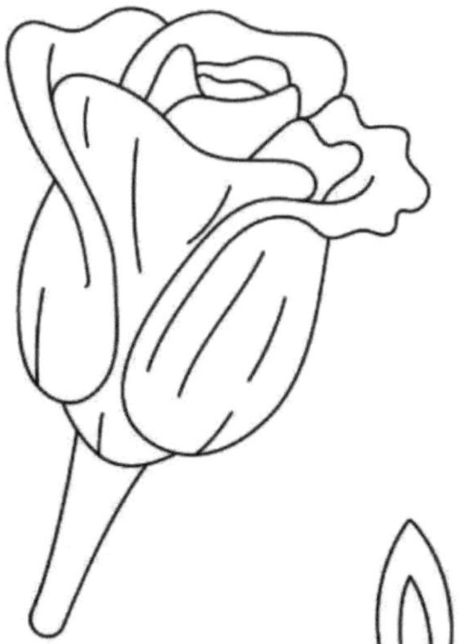

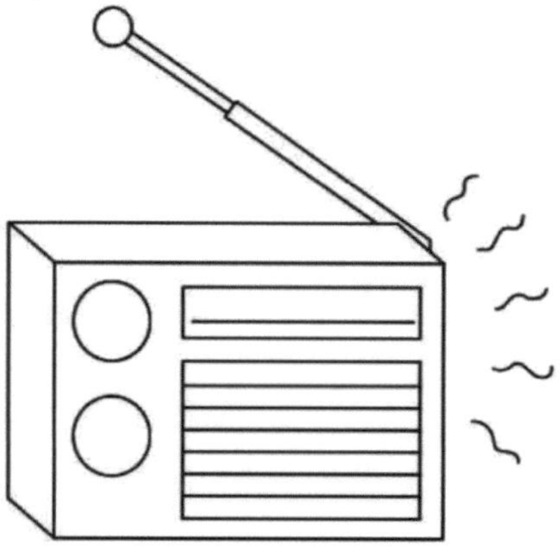

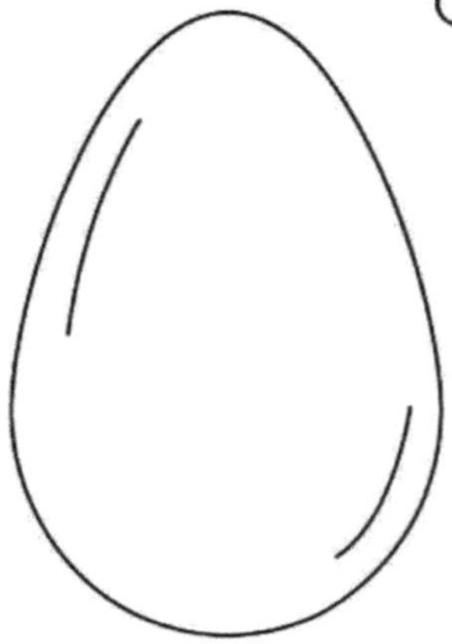

Trace the letters.

R R R R R R R R R R R R

r r r r r r r r r r r r

Wednesday

Direction: Color each object that start with the letter Oo.

Trace the letters.

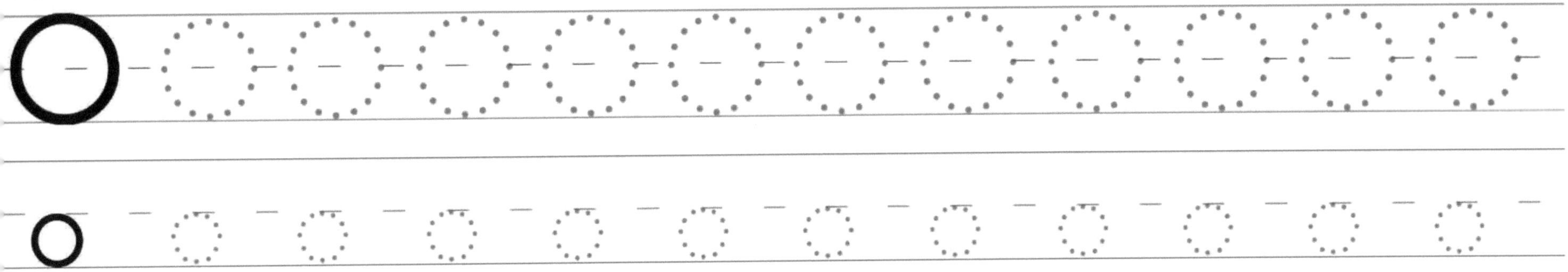

Thursday

Direction: Color each object that start with the letter Dd.

Trace the letters.

Thursday

Direction: Color each object that start with the letter Ii.

Trace the letters.

Friday

Direction: Color each object that start with the letter Tt.

Trace the letters.

Friday

Direction: Color each object that start with the letter Uu.

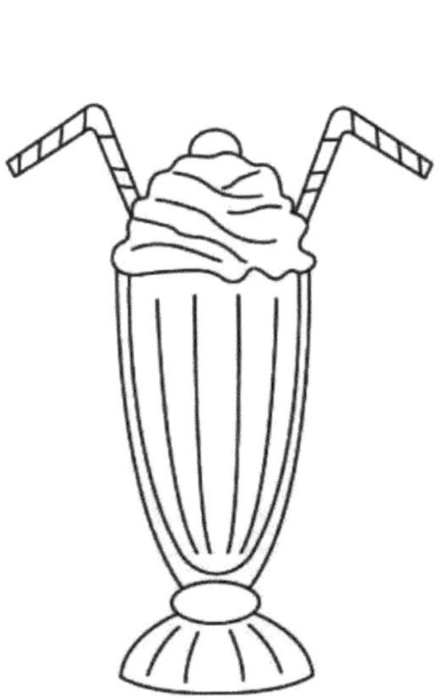

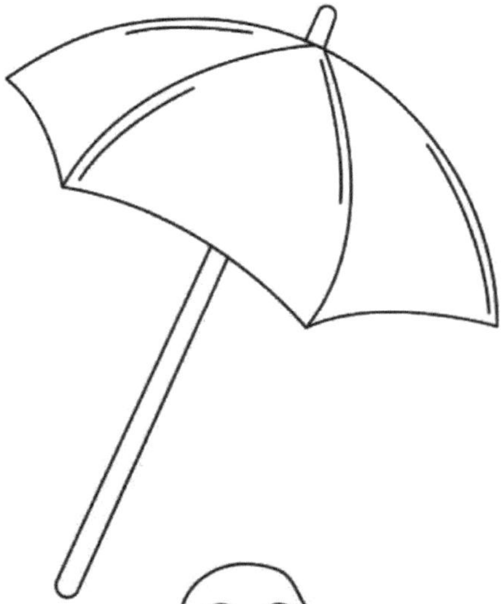

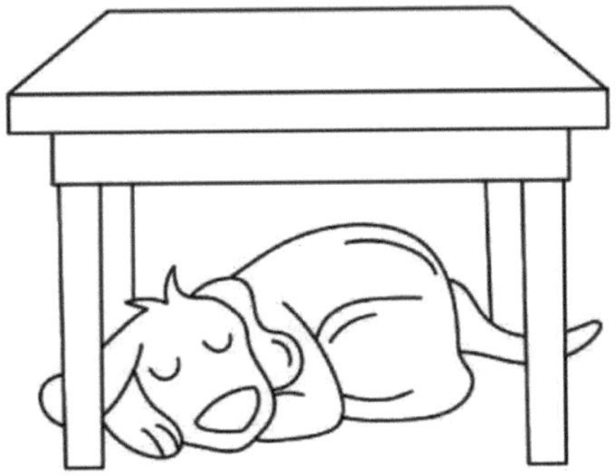

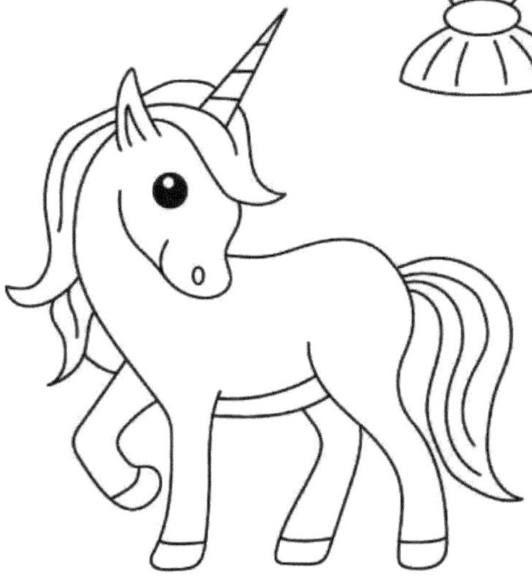

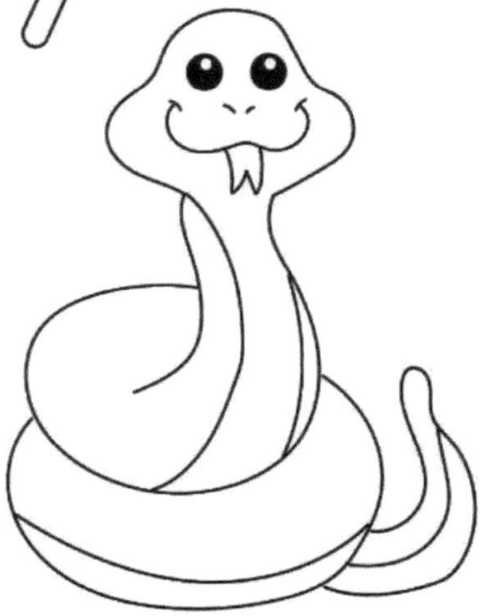

Trace the letters.

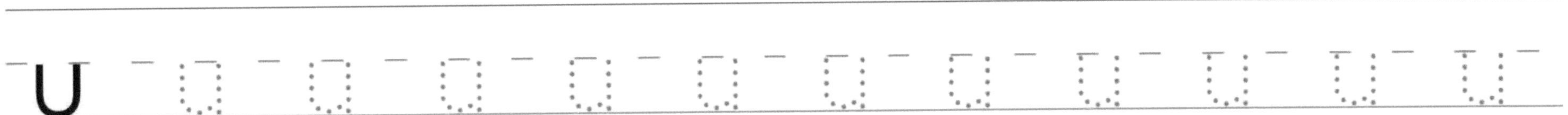

Word Search

Snacks

Apple
Candy
Ice Cream

Banana
Grapes
Popcorn

Yogurt
Donuts
Pudding

Oranges
Milk
Brownies

```
A S F H T V M H G L S V T J O S
X W Q T Y U I O C H Z D V T E G
I E D A P P L E L K J S H P V S
O R J L Y U K G Z B Q E A F C T
B R O W N I E S R T T Y R J H J
T Z Q H U E C S Z T G H L Y X C
D K N I C F C R E A M D W X Y K
M O E U C F P J R T Y O G U R O
N Z N E V U L U E T K R B W X T
A C V U N T M H Z D Q E T Y N L
C S G J T F C R K D O A E F G O
C E R O I S J J L V I F J W H R
A F C N F V R T F Y K F N I A A
N X S P T B A N A N A N D G L K N
D R T E A D F G Q W R L V C X G
Y X P O P C O R N J L N G J T S
```

Ealia cannot find her way to school. Will you show her the way to school?
SCHOOL

Ealia wants a book to read. Will you help her find the library?
LIBRARY

Color by Numbers

Direction: Color each space according to the number.

1. White

2. Yellow

3. Blue

4. Red

5. Pink

6. Purple

7. Orange

8. Brown

9. Grey

10. Green

Counting Sets

Directions: Count each set.
Write the number in the box.

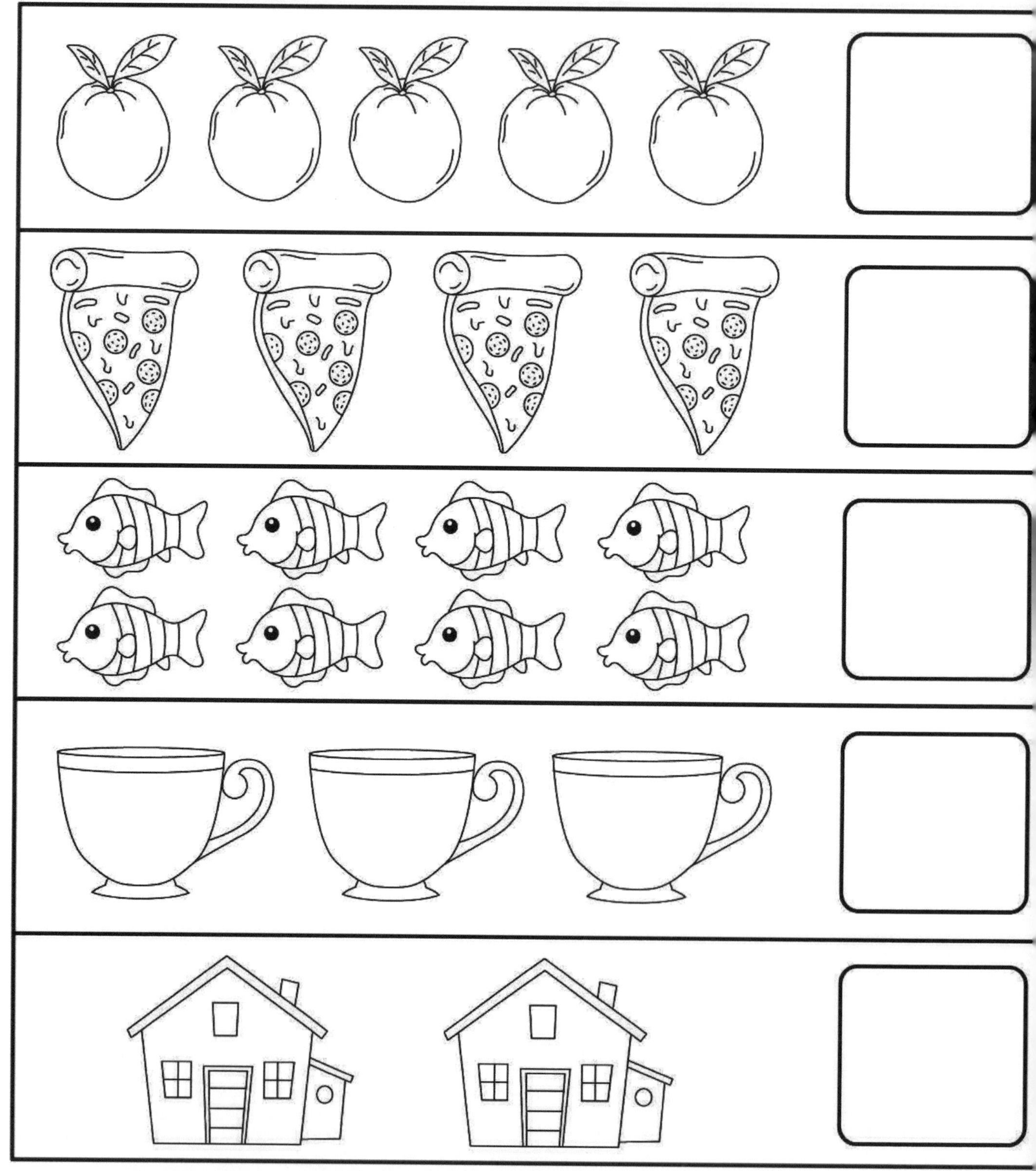

Counting Sets

Directions: Count each set.
Color the number in the set.

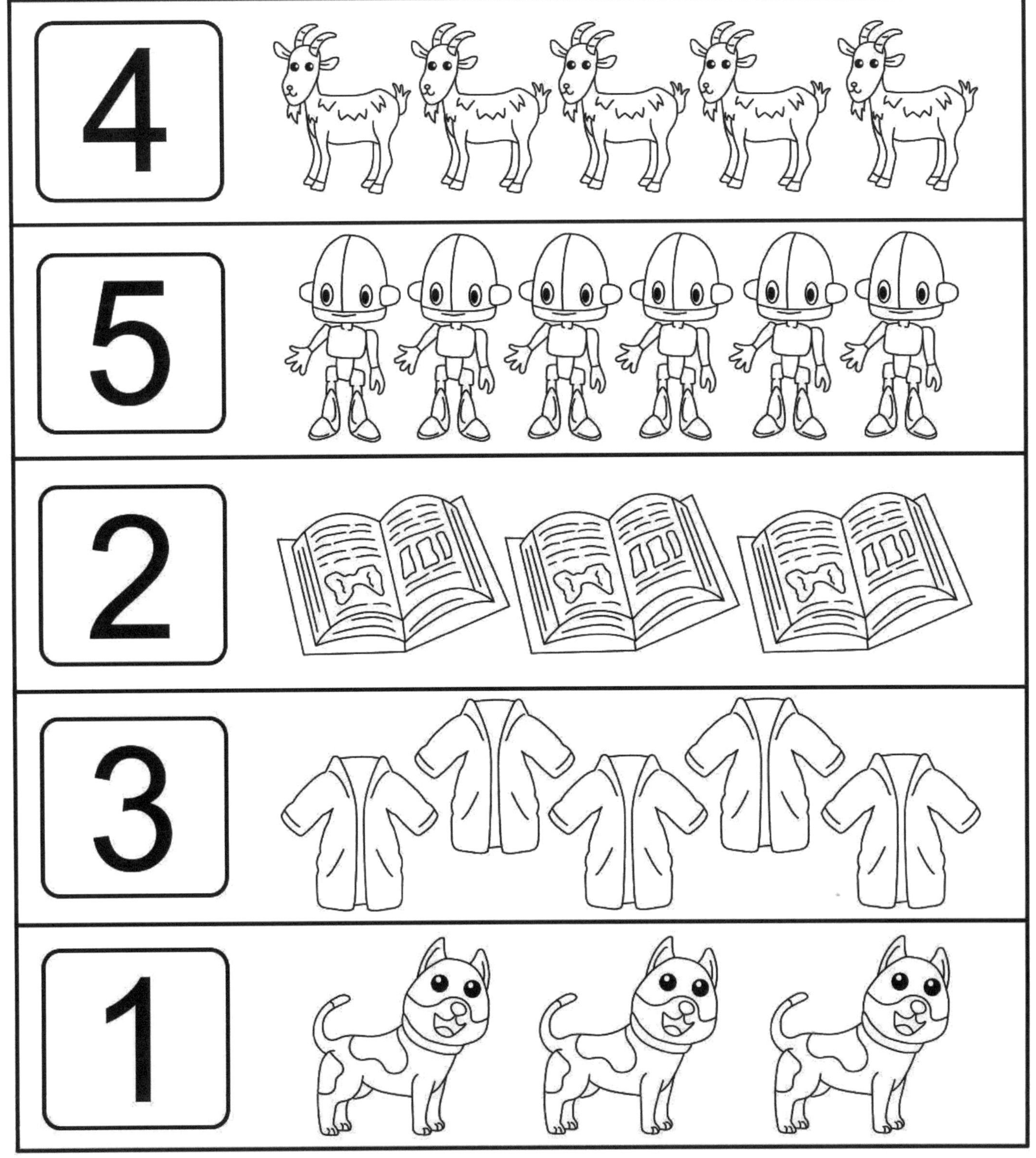

Counting Sets

Directions: Count each set.
Write the number in the box.

Counting Sets

Directions: Count each set.
Color the number in the set.

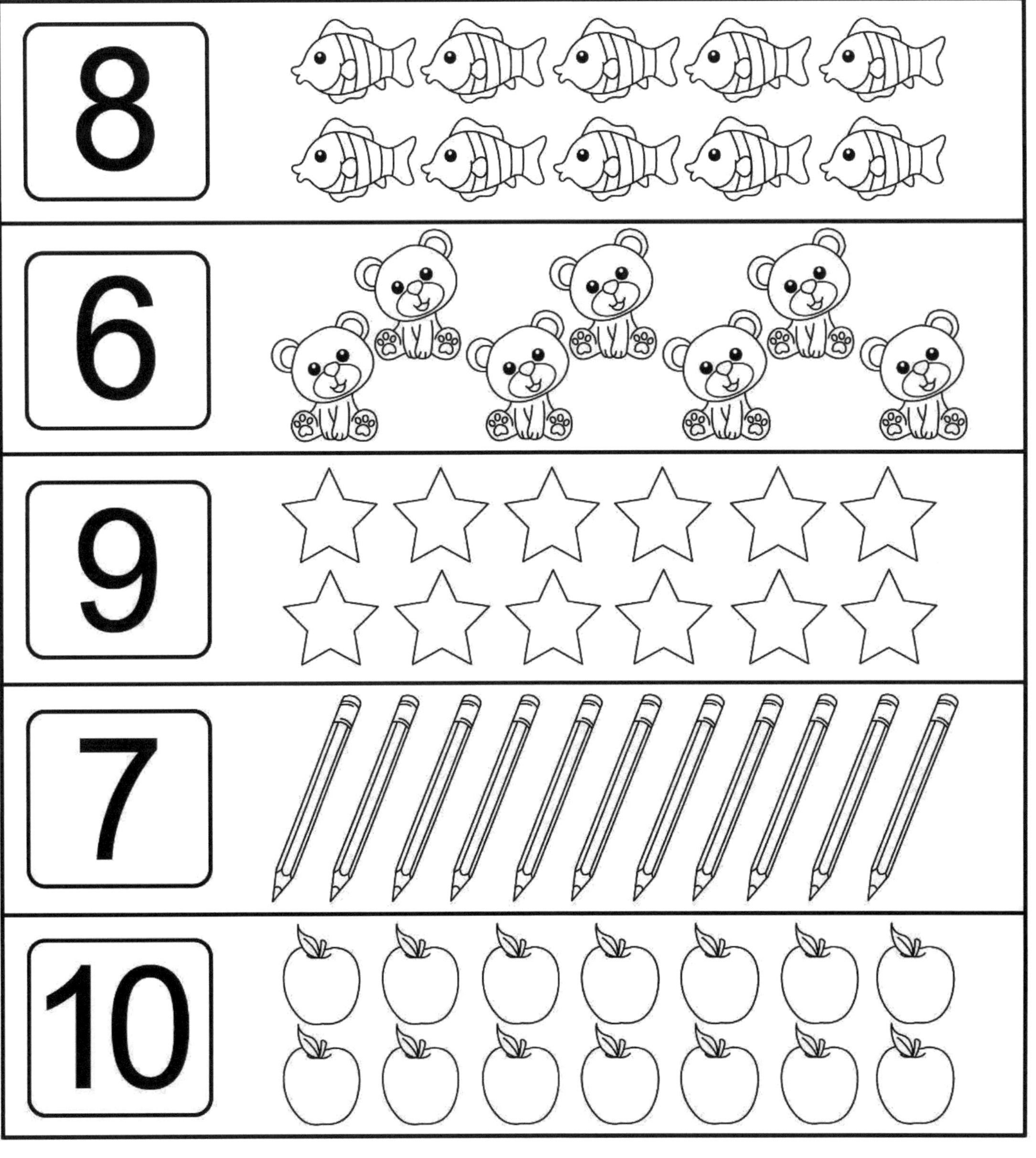

Number Chart 1 to 100

1									
									30
				55					
	72								
							88		
									100

Direction: Fill in the missing numbers.

Addition

Color the picture using the color code for the sum

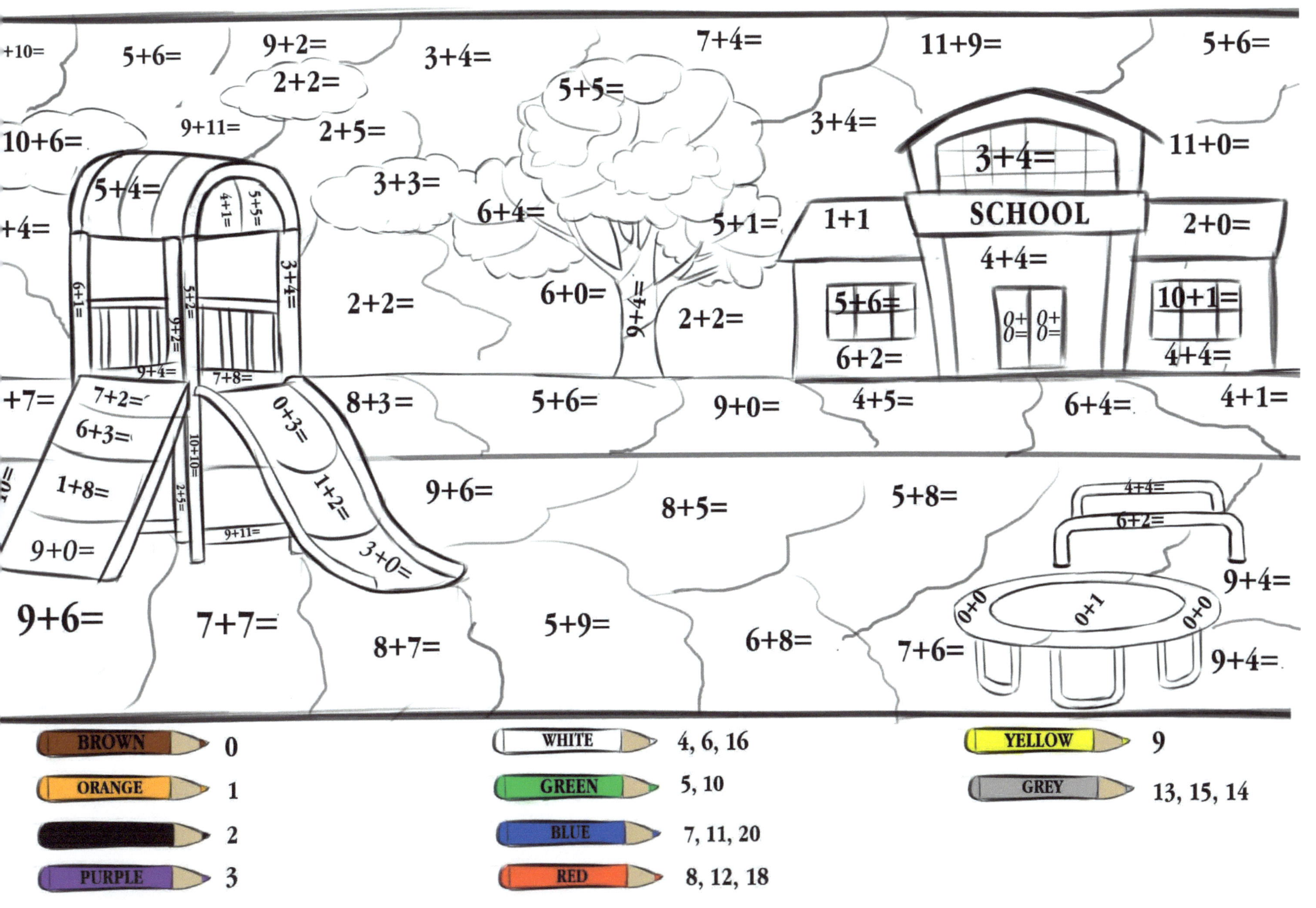

Color by Addition & Subtraction

Solve the problems with addition or subtraction. Use the color key code below to color the sum or difference.

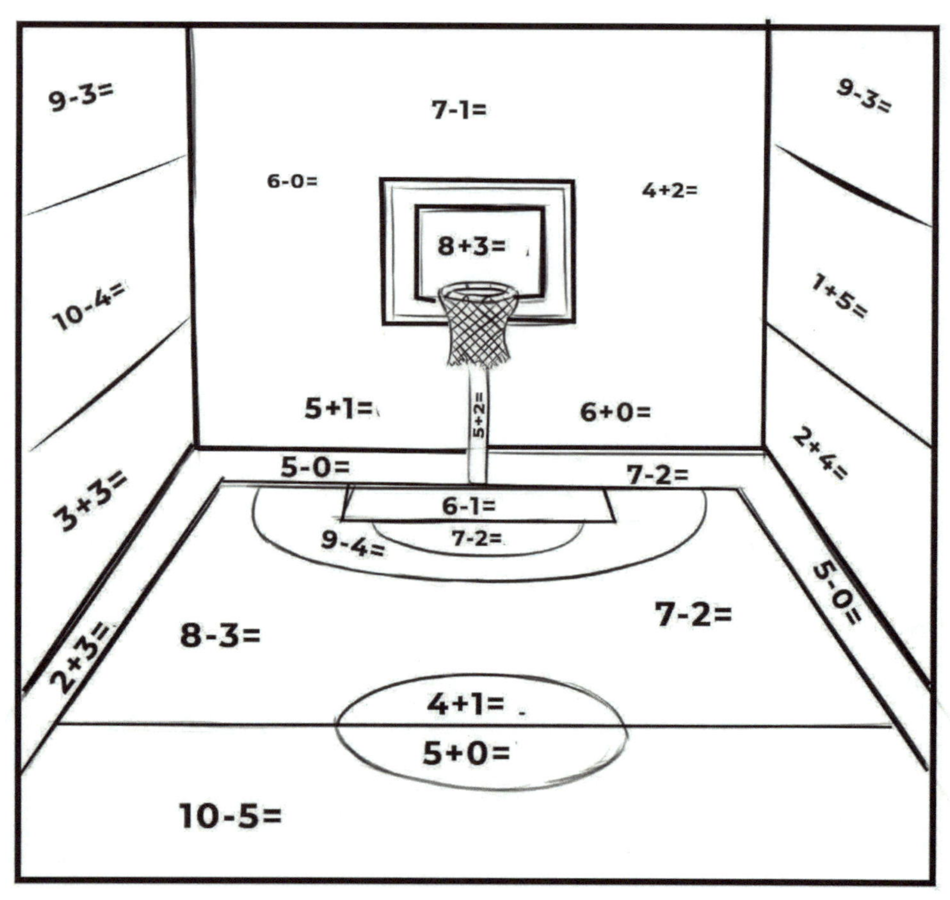

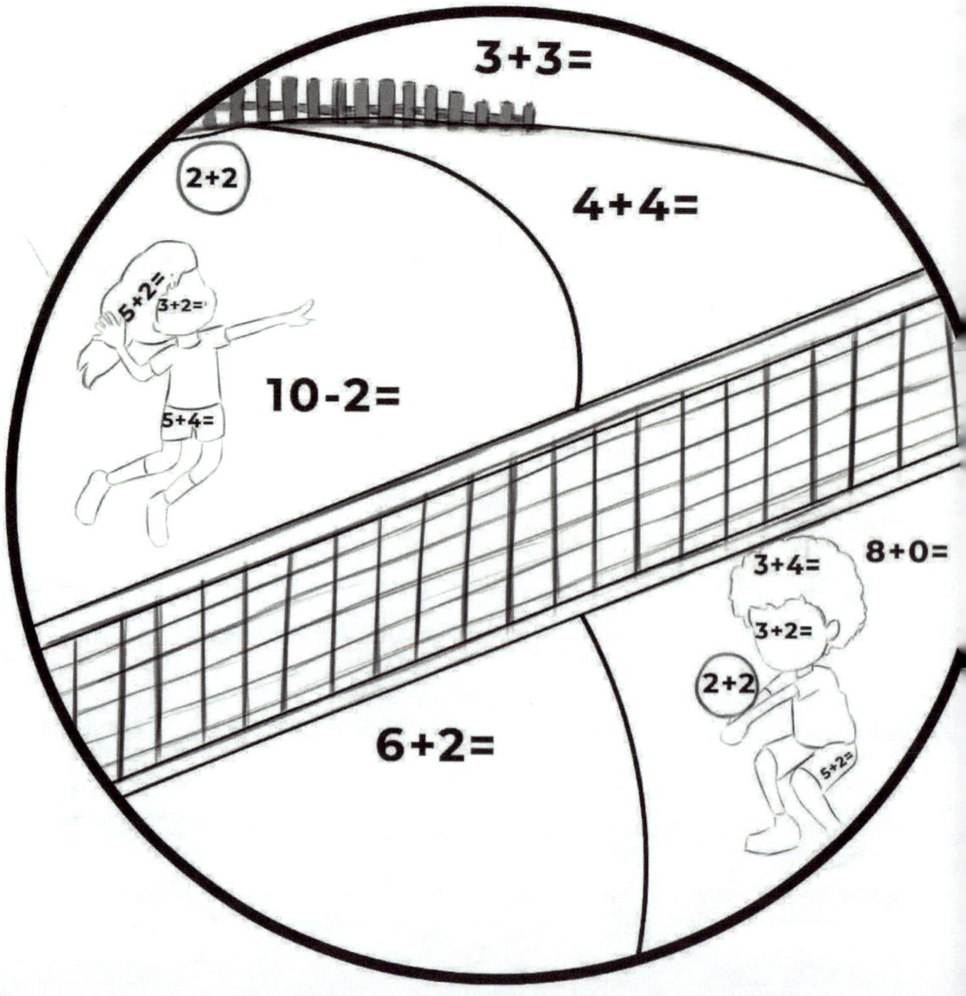

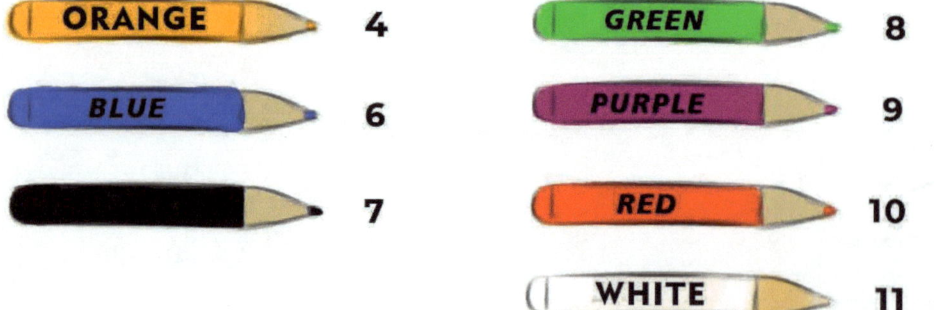

ORANGE	4	GREEN 8
BLUE	6	PURPLE 9
(black)	7	RED 10
		WHITE 11